go girl

Boy
Friend?

hardie grant EGMONT

Boy Friend?
first published in 2005
this edition published in 2011 by
Hardie Grant Egmont
Ground Floor, Building 1, 658 Church Street
Richmond, Victoria 3121, Australia
www.hardiegrantegmont.com.au

A CiP record for this title is available from the National Library of Australia

Text copyright © 2005 Meredith Badger
Illustration and design copyright © 2011 Hardie Grant Egmont

Illustration by Aki Fukuoka
Design by Michelle Mackintosh
Text design and typesetting by Ektavo

Printed in Australia by Griffin Press, an Accredited ISO AS/NZS
14001:2004 Environmental Management System printer.

3 5 7 9 10 8 6 4

The paper this book is printed on is certified against the
Forest Stewardship Council® Standards. Griffin Press holds
FSC chain of custody certification SGS-COC-005088. FSC
promotes environmentally responsible, socially beneficial
and economically viable management of the world's forests

Boy Friend?

by
Meredith Badger

Illustrations by
Aki Fukuoka

hardie grant EGMONT

Chapter One

'Come on, Mia!' called her mum from the front door. 'Time to go!'

'Coming!' Mia said, grabbing her school bag and rushing down the hallway.

Her older sister Rose was still in the kitchen, waiting for her friend Ashley to come over. They walked to high school together every day. Rose was concentrating on her mobile phone as Mia hurried by.

Probably sending text messages to James, Mia giggled to herself as she ran outside. Now that Rose had a boyfriend she seemed to be permanently glued to her phone!

Mia's brother Nick was already in the front seat when Mia jumped in the car. He was talking to Jack in the back seat.

Jack Pang lived next door to Mia's family. He was in Mrs Bonacci's class at school, just like Mia. Mia's mum often gave him a lift in the mornings.

'Hi, Jack!' said Mia, giving him a high-five.

'Hey, Mia!' said Jack, flashing her a cheeky grin.

'About time,' grumbled Nick. 'It's OK

for you *little* kids. We older ones get in trouble if we're late.'

Mia looked at Jack and rolled her eyes. Nick was only one grade ahead of her and Jack at school. But sometimes he acted like he thought he was way older!

Jack grinned at Mia. 'Don't worry, Grandpa,' he said, leaning forward to pat Nick gently on the back. 'We'll make sure you get to class on time. Would you like me to help you up the stairs, or did you remember your walking stick today?'

If I said something like that to Nick I'd be in BIG trouble! Mia thought to herself.

But Nick just grinned and gave Jack a pretend punch in the arm.

'Ha ha, very funny!' he said. 'I'm not *that* old!'

Mia grinned. *Jack's lucky he can get away with it!* she thought. *I guess that's one of the reasons I like him.*

It was funny. The Pang family had been living next door to Mia's family for as long as she could remember. But for ages Mia didn't know Jack very well. He'd always come over to hang out with Nick.

Mia used to stay out of their way. Nick was fun to hang out with when he was on his own. But Mia felt a bit shy around her brother's friends. They always seemed so loud and rough!

Mia's own friends from school — Michiko and Shae — didn't live walking distance from her house. So she hardly saw them outside school.

If only Jack was a girl, Mia used to sigh to herself when he came over to see Nick. *It'd be so nice to have a friend living right next door to me.*

But then a weird thing happened. Gradually Mia realised that Jack was really nice. They had lots of things in common! He liked the same kind of music that she liked. He was learning to surf, just like she was. And best of all, he loved playing ping-pong! In fact, he had way more things in common with *Mia* than with Nick.

Jack started coming over after school not to see Nick, but to play ping-pong with Mia in her family's shed. They started playing a huge ping-pong competition. Jack named it the 'Ping-Pong-A-Thon.'

'Whoever wins the most games out of one hundred will be the ping-pong champion,' Jack had announced.

So far, Jack had won twenty games and Mia had won twenty-five. It seemed like the more games they played, the better they both got at ping-pong. And the better friends she and Jack became!

Chapter Two

'Buckle up, everyone!' called Mia's mum, starting the car.

'All right!' said Jack. Then he grinned wickedly at Mia. 'Let's see if I can break my record today!'

Jack usually made Mia laugh within about a minute of the trip to school. It didn't matter what kind of mood Mia was in when she got into the car, she was always laughing by the time they got to the school gates. Now it had become a competition to see how long she could last before Jack made her crack up.

'Hey, Mia,' said Jack. 'What's this?'

He started swinging his arm wildly around in front of him. Then he did a funny little dance in his seat. He looked so silly that Mia could already feel the laughter burbling up in her throat.

'Um … ' she said, holding the laughter down. 'Do you need to go to the toilet, maybe?'

'No,' grinned Jack. 'This is what I'll look like winning the Ping-Pong-A-Thon! Woohoo!'

Mia burst out laughing.

'Hey, that's a record!' chuckled Jack. 'We haven't even left the driveway and I've made you laugh!'

'I'm not laughing because of your dance,' giggled Mia. 'I'm laughing at the idea of you beating me at ping-pong.'

'There's no way you'll beat Mia,' said Nick, turning around from the front seat. 'I hardly ever beat her and I'm almost two years older. She turns into Magic Mia when she's playing ping-pong. She never misses the ball!'

Mia felt good when Nick said that. Sometimes he acted like she was annoying. It was nice to hear him call her Magic Mia.

'Well, *she* might be Magic Mia,' said Jack, whacking invisible ping-pong balls around the car. 'But *I'm* Ping-Pong Pang, the Ping-Pong King!'

Ping-Pong Pang?

Mia burst out laughing again. Nick chuckled too.

'Yes!' said Jack, punching the air. 'I made you both laugh and we're still in our street.'

Then a song came on the radio that both Mia and Jack liked. Jack started singing. He had a great voice. To start with he sang the real words to the song. But then Mia realised he was making up his own words.

'I know this girl Mi-AH, well she lives in a tree-AH!'

There was no way Mia was letting Jack get away with that!

'You know that boy Jack-O, well he is really whack-O!' Mia sang even louder than Jack, to drown him out.

Nick shoved his fingers in his ears. 'Mum, I'm going to need some earplugs for when these two are together,' he groaned.

Their mum laughed. 'I can't believe Mrs Bonacci thinks you're shy, Mia,' she said. 'If she could hear you right now she wouldn't think that at all!'

Jack turned and looked at Mia. 'How come you're sometimes shy and sometimes not?' he said.

Mia shrugged. She wasn't really sure why. She just was. It was like the moment she walked into class she turned into someone else. It also happened when she was around people she didn't know very well. She often knew exactly what she *wanted* to say. But somehow the words got lost on their way out.

At school some kids called her Mouse because she was so quiet. Mia hated that nickname! She didn't feel like a mouse inside. But being teased just made her even more shy.

Mia's mum stopped the car out the front of their school. Waiting near the front gate were Shae and Michiko.

Mia smiled. Michiko was swinging on the gate as usual, which was against the rules.

I bet Shae's warning her to get off before she gets in trouble! thought Mia.

Shae and Michiko were really different to each other. And Mia was different to both of them. But they also had lots of things in common.

Mia looked across at Jack. Lots of things about him reminded her of Michiko and Shae. He liked reading adventure books like Shae. And he was good at doing handstands like Michiko.

Jack would get along really well with Michiko and Shae, decided Mia. But at school Jack played with his group and Mia played with hers. If a boy and a girl played together, everyone thought they *liked* each other.

It's a pity, Mia sighed, getting out of the car. *It'd be so cool if we were all friends!*

Chapter Three

Jack and Nick both spotted their friends and raced off to join them. Mia walked over to Michiko and Shae. She had the crazy song Jack had made up in her head.

'Hi, Mia!' called Michiko, hanging upside down over the gate. Michiko had just started going to circus classes and she was always practising her latest tricks. 'What are you smiling about?'

'Oh, just this silly song Jack made up this morning,' replied Mia, grinning. 'It was so funny.'

Shae leant against the fence, watching the boys disappear across the front lawn.

'You know, Jack looks a bit like Jesse McCartney,' she said.

Mia laughed. 'No he doesn't!' she said. 'Jack's got black hair, for one thing.'

'But he's got green eyes like Jesse. And the same hairstyle. Ella thinks he's cute.'

Mia didn't know what to say. She'd never thought of Jack as being cute before. He was just Jack.

'Hey, watch this!' said Michiko. She held onto the gate and then flipped her legs carefully over her head. Mia watched her friend admiringly. Michiko made it look so easy!

'Can you show me how to do that?' Mia asked.

'Sure!' said Michiko.

'Uh, Mia,' said Shae nervously. 'You're not supposed to swing on the gate. I've been telling Mich that all morning.'

'Don't worry, Shae,' said Michiko. 'We'll be quick. No-one will catch us.'

Michiko showed Mia how to hook her legs over the gate. But just as Mia was about to somersault off the gate, Brooke walked through. Brooke was in Mrs Bonacci's class, too. Mia almost accidentally kicked her.

'Careful, Mouse,' Brooke said crossly.

Mia flushed. 'Sorry,' she whispered.

'Well, you should be!' said Brooke huffily hurrying past.

Whoops!

Michiko stuck her tongue out and crossed her eyes as Brooke walked off. Shae waggled her fingers in her ears. Mia laughed. It was pretty babyish behaviour, but it was funny, too. Her friends always made her feel better.

'Hey, guess what!' said Shae, her eyes sparkling. 'I've got some goss about Brooke. She's got a boyfriend!'

'Really!' said Mia. 'Who?'

Shae looked around to check no-one was listening. 'Oliver Radcliffe!'

Oliver was in Jack's gang of friends, along with Flynn and Hugo. He had nice brown eyes and a big smile.

Mia knew lots of girls liked him. All

the same, she was surprised by Shae's goss. 'Are you sure?' she asked doubtfully. 'I've never even seen them talk to each other.'

'That doesn't matter,' said Shae. 'They've liked each other for ages.'

'How can you tell that?' asked Mia curiously.

Shae grinned. 'I can *always* tell,' she said. 'There are all these little give-aways. Like, some people check their hair a lot when they've got a crush on someone. Others get really clumsy or really shy. And some people just totally ignore the person they like!'

Mia laughed. She wasn't sure if she believed Shae. It sounded too weird.

Why would anyone want to ignore the person they liked?

'It's true!' insisted Shae. 'I can tell you who everyone in our class likes. For instance, I know Cassie likes Sam and Adrian likes Bec.'

'Who do *I* like then, Smartypants?' asked Michiko, grinning.

'That's easy,' said Shae. 'You like Flynn!'

Michiko went bright red. 'No I don't!' she said. 'I don't like anyone!'

Shae chuckled cheekily. 'You do *so* like Flynn. You always wave at him when he walks in the room. Plus he's the first boy you pick if you're team captain.'

Michiko gave Shae a friendly push. 'That just means I like him. It doesn't mean I *like* like him!' she said. 'Anyway, *you* obviously like Jack!'

Shae shrugged. 'Jack is nice,' she said. 'But there's someone who likes him *heaps* more than I do.'

'Do you mean Ella?' asked Mia. Ella was always talking to Jack.

Shae laughed. 'No, I meant *you*, Mia!'

Mia felt a blush creep up her neck, over her cheeks and then rush towards her ears. 'I do *not*!' she said.

'Yes, you do,' teased Shae. 'It's totally obvious he's your boyfriend. You're always talking about how funny and cool Jack is.

And he likes you, too. He's always smiling at you!'

Mia shook her head. 'He's not my *boyfriend*,' she insisted. 'He's my ...' Mia stopped for a moment. 'He's just my friend who's a boy ... my *friend-boy*!' she said eventually.

'Boyfriend, friend-boy — it's the same thing!' giggled Shae.

'No it's not!' said Mia. 'Jack is my friend like you guys are my friends.'

'*Sure* he is!' chuckled Michiko. 'We believe you!'

Just then the bell rang. Mia had never been so happy to hear it in her life. This conversation was just way too embarrassing.

'Come on!' said Michiko, dashing off. 'I'll race you both to class!'

Mia ran after Michiko. It was nice to be distracted from all the thoughts swirling around in her head.

Still, she couldn't help wondering.

Jack was a friend. And he was a boy. Did that mean he was actually her *boyfriend*?

Michiko and Shae seemed to think so!

Chapter Four

Mia, Michiko and Shae made it to their classroom just before the second bell rang. Mia looked around at everyone in her class, remembering what Shae had said about who liked who.

She noticed Adrian playing with his fringe when Bec walked by. Then Cassie went bright red when Sam said hi. And on Brooke's pencil case was a love heart with the letters O.R. written inside!

The door opened and Flynn entered, late as usual. Mia couldn't help grinning as Michiko looked up and gave him a wave!

Maybe Shae does *know everyone's secret crushes!* thought Mia. Then she started feeling weird. If Shae was right about everyone else, was she right about Jack, too?

Mia looked around. Jack was up the back, chatting with Hugo. He saw her looking at him and crossed his eyes and gave her a big smile.

Jack does smile at me a lot, realised Mia. *Maybe he* does *have a crush on me!*

Suddenly Mia's stomach did a flip. She liked Jack a lot. But just as a friend.

'OK, class,' said Mrs Bonacci, clapping her hands to start the class. 'Can anyone tell me what a friend is?'

Straight away lots of people put their hands in the air. But Mia scrunched down into her chair. She really didn't want to be chosen!

'Cassie,' said Mrs Bonacci. 'What do you think a friend is?'

'Someone who is exactly the same as you?' said Cassie.

Then Michiko put up her hand. 'I don't think a friend needs to be *exactly* the same as you, Mrs Bonacci,' she said. 'Shae, Mia and I are really different but we're still best friends.'

Mrs Bonacci smiled. 'Great answer,' she said, looking around at the class. 'What about you, Mia? Tell us what you like most about your friends.'

Everyone turned and stared at Mia. Straight away she felt her face getting hot and red.

Mia thought hard. There were heaps of fantastic things about her friends. She wanted to tell everyone about how funny her friends were, and how loyal. And how special she felt when she was around them. But when Mia opened her mouth, nothing came out!

Mia shook her head quickly, feeling tears in her eyes.

'Don't worry, Mia,' said Mrs Bonacci gently. 'You'll have another chance to tell us later.'

Mia flushed, feeling so embarrassed. Michiko and Shae grabbed her hands, and gave them a squeeze. Mia felt a little better, and smiled gratefully at them.

'The reason that we're discussing friendship,' said Mrs Bonacci, turning to the rest of the class, 'is because we are going to make a friendship time capsule.'

Straight away, Michiko asked the question everyone was thinking. 'What's a friendship time capsule?'

Mrs Bonacci pointed to a large glass jar on her desk. 'That's one there!' she said.

Everyone stared at the jar. There didn't seem to be anything very special about it, except that it was very big.

'It's just a *jar* at the moment, of course,' smiled Mrs Bonacci, as if she was reading their minds. 'It's our job to turn it into a time capsule. Your homework over the weekend is to write a tribute to your friends. Then on Monday we will put the tributes into this jar and bury it somewhere in the school grounds.'

Michiko rolled her eyes at Mia. 'Homework over the weekend ... yuck!' she whispered.

'I know,' Mia whispered back, 'but at least it sounds sort of fun.'

Flynn put up his hand. 'Mrs Bonacci, what's a tribute?' he asked.

'It's a piece of writing that explains why we think someone or something is special,' explained Mrs Bonacci. 'Before we bury the time capsule, we will read our tributes out loud so everyone can hear why we like our friends.'

Mia felt her heart thump in her chest. She really wanted to write a tribute, but she wasn't sure if she would be able to read in front of everyone. She tried to push the thought aside. *I'll worry about that later,* she decided.

'How long will the time capsule be buried for?' asked Bec.

Mrs Bonacci looked around. 'What does everyone think?' she said.

'We could dig it up on our last day of primary school,' suggested Shae.

Mrs Bonacci nodded. 'Perfect.'

'Can we decorate our tributes?' asked Jamie.

'Definitely!' said Mrs Bonacci. 'And you can include photos, too.'

This is going to be cool!

Even though Mia was nervous about having to read in front of everyone, she was excited, too. It was going to be cool doing this time capsule. And she could tell by looking around that everyone else felt the same way.

Chapter Five

At recess, Mia, Shae and Michiko grabbed their drinks and snacks and went to their favourite bench by the oval.

'I'm *sooo* excited about the time capsule,' said Shae, peeling her mandarin and offering the wedges around. 'Let's put in heaps of photos.'

'Hey!' said Michiko suddenly. 'We don't have any photos of us together from this year yet! Only that blurry one from when Mia tried to teach us to surf in my backyard.'

'You're right,' Shae nodded. 'We need some new ones. Who's got a camera?'

'Ours is broken,' sighed Michiko.

'We've got a digital camera,' said Mia. 'But I'm not allowed to bring it to school.'

Shae shrugged. 'That's OK,' she said. 'Can we come to your house on Saturday? The time capsule isn't being buried until Monday, so we've got heaps of time.'

'Sure!' said Mia, feeling excited. It felt like ages since Michiko and Shae had been to her house. 'Maybe we could dress up for the photos. You know – like a proper photo shoot?'

'Great idea!' said Michiko. 'We could dress up like clowns – I've got some cool wigs we could wear, and some face paint.'

'Maybe,' said Shae doubtfully. Then she started rummaging around in her pocket. 'Actually, why don't we ask … this!' She pulled out what looked like a piece of paper folded into triangles.

'What's that?' asked Michiko. 'It looks like origami.'

'It's a fortune teller,' explained Shae. 'My sister showed me how to make one last night. It helps you make decisions. And it can predict the future!'

She poked her thumbs and forefingers up into the points of the four triangles. Mia noticed that written on the outside of the triangles were the numbers one to eight.

Shae held the fortune teller out to Michiko.

'Ask it a yes or no question, Mich,' she instructed.

'OK,' said Michiko. 'Should we dress up as clowns for the photo shoot?'

'Now, pick a number,' said Shae.

Michiko picked three.

'One, two, three,' counted Shae, moving the triangles back and forth with her fingers. Then she held the fortune teller out to Michiko again. Written inside it were the words red, blue, orange and green. Michiko picked red.

'R, E, D,' said Shae, moving the triangles again as she spelt out the colour. Now the choices were yellow, purple, pink and aqua. Michiko chose aqua.

Shae unfolded the flap to read what was written underneath. 'It says *Bad idea!*' she laughed.

Michiko didn't seem to mind. 'That thing is so cool!' she said. 'Ask it something else.'

Shae thought for a moment. Then she smiled her cheekiest smile. 'Does Mia have a crush on Jack?' she said. She passed the fortune teller to Mia.

'I keep telling you. I *don't* have a crush on him!' laughed Mia. But all the same she felt her cheeks go pink. Jack and his gang were playing nearby. She really hoped they hadn't heard Shae!

'Let's see what the fortune teller has to say,' said Shae. 'If you don't have a crush, it'll tell us.'

What will it say?

Shae picked four, and Mia moved the fortune teller in and out, four times. Then Shae picked orange, then blue. Mia felt her heart skip a beat as she opened up the flap.

But before Mia could read the answer Michiko grabbed it out of her hands and read it with Shae. Then they both burst out laughing.

'Come on! Tell me what it says!' said Mia. 'Do I have a crush on him or not?'

'It says *There's no doubt about it!*' giggled Shae.

'Now ask it if Jack has a crush on Mia,' said Michiko.

So Shae asked the question. She chose two, then yellow. Then she chose yellow again, and Michiko opened up the flap.

'It says, *It's looking good*!' she laughed. 'You love Jack, Mia, and he loves you!'

Mia rolled her eyes. 'Just because a piece of paper says so doesn't mean it's true!' she said. 'I'm *positive* I don't have a crush on him.'

'Sorry, Mia,' grinned Shae. 'There's no point denying it!'

Chapter Six

Early on Saturday morning, Mia stretched out on the lounge room floor with a notebook and pen. She really wanted to write her tribute before Shae and Michiko came over for the photo shoot.

But it was hard to concentrate. The house was really noisy and crazy. Nick was practising the drums in his room. Rose was doing her homework and listening to music with the volume turned right up.

Mia sighed as she looked at her page. She'd barely written anything.

My friends are really great because

There was another problem, too. She knew that Michiko and Shae were her friends. But what about Jack? She had been so sure that they were just friends. What if Shae was right, and Jack did have a crush on her?

I don't think he has, thought Mia, chewing on her pen. *But how can you tell?*

Just then, Rose wandered into the lounge room and flopped onto the sofa. 'Whatcha doing?' she asked.

'Homework,' replied Mia. Then she had a thought. *Rose knows all about crushes!*

'Rose,' asked Mia, a little shyly. 'How can you tell if a boy likes you?'

Rose looked at her and smiled. 'Does someone have a crush on my baby sister?' she said.

'Uhh, it's not about me!' said Mia hastily. The last thing she needed was Rose teasing her as well! 'I'm asking for a friend of mine.'

'Sure, I understand,' grinned Rose. 'Well, is this boy nicer to your *friend* than to other girls?'

Mia thought about it. 'I guess so,' she said. 'They get along pretty well.'

'Does he pay her lots of attention?' asked Rose.

Mia frowned. 'What do you mean?'

'Well, does he look at her a lot?' explained Rose.

'All the time!' Mia nodded. 'But mostly to make her laugh while the teacher is talking.'

'Doesn't matter,' said Rose. 'He's still staring. Does he give her compliments?'

'Um ... ' Mia thought hard. Jack was

always telling her how good she was at ping-pong. That was a compliment. 'Yes, he does,' said Mia.

Rose grinned. 'I'd say the boy definitely had a crush on your friend,' she said.

'Oh,' said Mia. *Maybe it's true,* she thought. *Everyone else seems to think so.*

Oh no!

Then Mia jumped up. She didn't want to talk about crushes anymore. 'If anyone is looking for me I'll be in the shed!' she called, escaping out the back door.

The shed was Mia's favourite place. It was kind of like another lounge room, but just for kids. In one half was the ping-pong table. In the other was an old sofa and a CD player. It was the best place to think.

When she arrived at the shed she got a big surprise. Jack was sitting on the step, twirling his ping-pong paddle between his hands.

'Hi!' he said. 'I knocked at your house, but no-one answered. What's going on in there?'

'Everything!' groaned Mia. 'You can hear Nick and his drums from here!'

'Feel like playing ping-pong?' asked Jack.

'OK,' Mia said, racing into the shed and grabbing her paddle. 'Get ready!'

Pow! The ball flew over the net and Jack leapt up, just managing to hit it back. This game was super close. Jack would win a shot and then Mia would win the next one. But then Jack hit the ball so that it bounced on the opposite corner to where Mia was standing. There was no way she could get to it in time, and the ball zoomed past.

Jack did a pivot and punched the air. 'Finally!' he said. 'I was beginning to think I'd never beat you again. You're way too good at ping-pong.'

Suddenly, Mia felt nervous. *I should just ask him if he's got a crush on me,* she thought. *Then we can sort this out once and for all!*

'Um, Jack?' said Mia. 'I've got a question.' Her cheeks felt hot.

Jack had dropped to the floor and was looking under the table for the spare ball. 'What?' he asked.

Mia squirmed. This was going to be hard! 'Do you —'

'Hey, Mia,' Nick called, poking his head inside the shed and tapping his drumsticks on the door. 'Your friends are out the front.'

'Oh! Thanks,' said Mia, putting down her paddle. 'See you later, Jack.'

She couldn't help feeling relieved. The big question would have to wait!

Chapter Seven

'Hi, Mia!' called Michiko.

She and Shae were walking down the driveway. Shae was carrying a huge bag over her shoulder.

'What's in that?' asked Mia curiously.

'Heaps of Georgia's costumes,' said Shae. Shae's sister Georgia did drama, and she had lots of outfits from the plays she'd been in. 'We can use them for the photo shoot.'

'Where should we go and get ready?' asked Michiko, looking around.

Mia thought for a moment. She could hear a game of ping-pong going on in the shed. Nick must have started playing a game with Jack.

'Let's go inside,' she suggested. She led her friends through the front door, stopping to grab the camera from the lounge room. Then they walked upstairs to the bedroom Mia shared with Rose. Rose's music was still blaring from the CD player.

Michiko and Shae looked around, admiring all of Rose's things.

'I *so* love The Veronicas,' Michiko said, pointing to one of Rose's many posters.

'Sometimes when I listen to them I pretend I'm in the band.'

'I do that, too!' admitted Shae with a grin. She started singing and pretending to play guitar, shaking her head so her long hair swished around. Then she looked at the others.

'I've got a great idea!' she said. 'We should dress up like a rock band for our photo shoot.'

'*Great* idea!' Michiko and Mia said together.

Shae started rifling through the huge bag of clothes. She tossed a red stripy dress and some black leggings at Michiko. Mia caught a floppy silver mini-tutu as it flew over her head. She pulled it on over her jeans and looked at herself in the mirror. The tutu looked very cute!

Shae slipped into a black top and a tartan skirt. 'Now, for the finishing touch,' she said, pulling a spray can out of the bag. 'Hair colour!'

'No way ... Mum will kill me!' said Mia, giggling and backing away.

'Don't worry,' said Shae. 'It washes out. And we'll just do one stripe each.'

Mia thought for a moment, and figured it would be OK. She let Shae take a small chunk of her hair and spray it with colour.

'Wow, Mia,' said Michiko, when Shae had finished. 'It looks amazing!'

Mia took another look in the mirror. Michiko was right – the pink stripe looked fantastic! She didn't look like Mia any more. She looked like a rock star! Having the pink stripe made her feel different somehow, too. She felt sort of braver.

I feel like a rock star!

'Me next!' said Michiko excitedly. So Shae gave her hair a stripe, too. Then she looked in the mirror, and added one in her own hair.

Once they all had a pink stripe, Mia grabbed the camera and held it out in front of them. 'Squish in tight!' she said. They all pulled funny faces and Mia took a photo.

'Now I feel like dancing!' said Michiko, doing a spin.

'Yeah, me too!' said Mia, turning the music up.

But just as they started dancing, Rose appeared in the doorway with her friend, Ashley.

'Sorry, guys,' she said. 'We've got homework to do in here.'

'But can't you work at the kitchen table?' asked Mia.

'No, we need privacy,' Rose replied.

Mia knew that meant that Rose and Ashley would probably just sit around talking about the boys that they liked. But there was no point arguing with her. Rose always won!

'Come on,' Mia said to Michiko and Shae, grabbing the camera. 'Let's go to the shed. There's an old CD player in there.'

Jack and Nick were still playing ping-pong when Mia and her friends opened the shed door. The ball was flying back and forth at top speed!

Mia put on one of Rose's CDs and started dancing around. Michiko and Shae joined in too. As she spun around, Mia saw Nick rolling his eyes. She grinned, and then grabbed an old broom to use as a microphone. She swished her hair and sang as loudly as she could.

'Wow, Mia,' laughed Michiko. 'If Brooke could see you now, she'd never call you Mouse again!'

'That reminds me,' giggled Shae, trying to catch her breath. 'I heard that Brooke and

Oliver have broken up. And guess what —
she likes Hugo now.'

Mia realised that the sound of the
ping-pong game had stopped. She turned
around. Jack and Nick were leaning against
the table, listening in.

'Hey,' called Jack. 'Would you like to
know who *I've* got a crush on?'

'Uh … yes!' said Shae. 'Who?'

Mia looked at Jack. Suddenly she felt a
bit nervous. What was he going to say?

Chapter Eight

'You have to guess,' grinned Jack.

'Give us some clues then,' said Michiko, glancing at Mia. 'Is she sporty?'

'Well, she loves playing ping-pong,' said Jack.

'What does she look like?' asked Shae.

'She's little and cute,' said Jack. 'And her face is really red.'

Mia stared at Jack. *Is he talking about me?*

She put her hands up to her cheeks. Her face was definitely red right now! And she was the smallest girl in Mrs Bonacci's class.

Mia didn't know what to think. *It* has *to be me Jack's talking about,* worried Mia.

Please don't say my name!

She couldn't help feeling that everything would change if she found out that he had a crush on her. Jack was really smart and nice. He was very funny, too. And she knew that other girls thought he was cute. But Mia was happy with things just the way they were.

I really hope that Jack doesn't *have a crush on me,* realised Mia. *I just want us to be normal friends!*

Everyone was looking curiously at Jack now, even Nick.

'Is it someone who we know?' asked Michiko.

'Actually, she's in the room with us right now!' said Jack, grinning broadly.

'Just *tell* us!' groaned Shae.

Mia was so nervous about what Jack would say, she felt like running out of the shed. She pretended to be very interested in the silver tutu she was wearing.

Then suddenly Michiko, Shae and Nick burst out laughing. Mia looked up.

Jack was holding up his red ping-pong paddle. On it he had drawn a big smiling face.

'This is Paula Paddle,' he said. 'Isn't she beautiful?'

'Are you saying you've got a crush on your ping-pong paddle?' giggled Michiko.

Jack pretended to look hurt. 'So?' he said. 'What's wrong with that?'

'Yeah!' chuckled Nick. 'Jack can like whoever he wants. Even if she's a ping-pong paddle!'

'But she's made out of wood!' Shae laughed.

'I don't care!' said Jack. 'I like her anyway.' Then he gave the paddle a big smoochy kiss.

Mia started laughing, too. She couldn't believe Jack had just kissed his ping-pong paddle! She also felt very relieved.

I'm so glad Jack doesn't have a crush on me, she thought happily.

'Wait a minute,' Shae said, looking at Jack through narrowed eyes. 'Are you sure you don't like anyone *else*?'

Jack looked surprised. 'Like who?'

'Like Mia!' said Michiko.

'Sorry, but no,' Jack said, shaking his head. 'Just because Mia and I are buddies doesn't mean we *like* like each other.'

'Yeah,' added Mia. 'We're just really good friends.'

Michiko nodded. Mia could tell she

understood. But Shae still didn't seem to believe them.

'Let's ask the fortune teller again,' said Shae, pulling it out of her pocket and slotting in her fingers. 'Do Jack and Mia have crushes on each other?'

'This is so dumb!' laughed Jack. But he sighed, and went along with it anyway. First he chose four, then green, and finally purple.

Mia held her breath as Shae unfolded the flap.

'So?' said Michiko. 'What does it say?'

'It says *No way!*' admitted Shae, looking disappointed. 'But I don't believe it. I was *sure* you guys *like* liked each other.'

'It's just a silly fortune teller!' Mia said.

Jack shook his head, half-laughing, half-serious. 'It *is* possible for a boy and a girl to be just friends, OK?' he said. 'Mia's cool and I like hanging out with her. She's funny and really smart, too. It makes no difference to me that she's a girl and not a boy.'

For a moment no-one said anything.

Then Michiko smiled. 'That's so nice.'

'Yeah,' Shae nodded. 'Now I believe you. Only a real friend would say something like that.'

Mia smiled, feeling a bit shy all of a sudden. She knew that Jack liked her as a friend. But she had never heard the reasons *why* he liked her. It was nice to hear. But it was also a bit embarrassing.

All the same, thought Mia happily, *I'm so glad he's my* friend!

Chapter
Nine

Michiko reached down and picked up a blue paddle lying on the floor.

'Hey, this paddle is quite cute, too!' she giggled. 'Hi, Peter Paddle! Is it OK if I use your head to play ping-pong with?' Then she made the paddle waggle up and down, like it was nodding.

'You know, I haven't played ping-pong for ages,' said Shae.

'Why don't we play rounders ping-pong?' suggested Nick.

Mia was surprised. Usually Nick acted like her friends were too boring for him to hang out with.

'What's that?' asked Michiko.

'It's cool!' said Jack. 'One person hits the ball over the net, drops the paddle and runs off to the side. Then the next person has to run over, grab the paddle and try to hit the ball.'

'So every shot is hit by a different person?' said Michiko.

'Exactly,' Nick nodded.

'Sounds fun,' said Shae, jumping up. 'Let's play!'

It was the weirdest game Mia had ever played. The moment one of them hit the ball over the net they had to run off to the side, to make room for the next person. Then they had to run to the other side of the net as quickly as they could. Mia found herself getting very puffed!

Shae kept missing the ball. 'I'm hopeless at this!' she said laughing, but looking frustrated.

'No you're not,' said Nick. 'You just need some coaching. Here, I'll show you.'

Mia stared at her brother in surprise. He never gave *her* any coaching! Nick showed Shae how to hit the ball so it was really difficult for anyone to hit it back. After that, Shae was much better.

'Your brother is really nice,' Shae whispered to Mia. Her cheeks were suddenly very pink!

They kept playing until everyone was too tired to run anymore. Then Nick threw his paddle down.

'I'm totally stuffed!' he groaned, flopping down onto the ground. Everyone else sat down, too.

'That was sooo fun!' said Michiko. 'We should play ping-pong at school some time. There's a table in the storeroom.'

'Great idea,' said Jack. 'I know Flynn would be into that. He loves ping-pong.'

'Really?' said Michiko. 'Hey, Jack … does Flynn have a crush on anyone?' she added, as if she didn't care either way.

Jack gave her a sly grin. 'I'm not telling you that!' he said. 'You'll have to find out for yourself if he likes you!'

'I didn't mean *me*,' said Michiko, blushing.

'*Sure* you didn't!' teased Shae.

Michiko looked at her watch. 'Hey!' she said, jumping up. 'Let's take some more photos. My mum will be here soon.'

Jack got up to leave. But Shae grabbed his arm.

'You have to be in at least one photo with us,' she insisted. 'You're Mia's friend, after all.'

Jack paused. 'Aren't we all friends now?' he said, pretending to be hurt.

'Of course we are!' said Michiko. 'Does that mean you'll be in a photo? Go on … say yes!'

Jack grinned cheekily. 'Not if it means I have to dye my hair pink!'

'That's OK,' Shae laughed. 'You can stay just as you are.'

Michiko, Shae, Mia and Jack posed in front of the ping-pong table, holding their paddles. Nick pointed the camera.

'Say sneeze!' he said.

'SNEEZE!' yelled everyone.

Mia could just tell it was going to be a great shot. One that would always remind her of this afternoon, playing with all of her friends.

And all of a sudden, Mia knew just what she should write for her friendship tribute.

Chapter Ten

Mrs Bonacci had told the class that they would bury the time capsule straight after lunch on Monday. The morning went really slowly for Mia. Even lunchtime seemed to drag by.

Jack came past on his way to join his friends. 'Hey, guys,' he said. 'Mr Perelli is going to set up the ping-pong table for us tomorrow.'

'Cool! I can't wait!' said Michiko excitedly.

'How funny,' chuckled Jack. 'That's exactly what Flynn said.'

'Is he going to play?' asked Michiko, fiddling with her hair.

'He was totally into the idea,' said Jack. 'Especially when he heard you'd be playing.'

Mia laughed at Michiko's red cheeks. It was kind of good to know she wasn't the only one who got embarrassed!

Just then, the bell rang. They all jumped off the bench.

'Finally!' Mia said happily. 'Come on!'

Mrs Bonacci's class met in the native garden beside the tuckshop.

Mrs Bonacci put the empty jar down. 'OK, who wants to go first?' she asked.

Mia's heart did a double-quick beat. This was the moment she'd been worrying about!

Michiko nudged her. 'Hey, Magic Mia, go for it!'

'Yeah,' whispered Shae, grinning. 'Are you a rock star or not?'

Mia's heart thumped. Her hands felt sweaty. She'd spent a lot of time decorating her tribute. There were drawings of flowers along the bottom edge and ping-pong paddles along the top. And she'd added swirls in the margins with her glitter pens.

She looked at the photo glued to the top. It was the one of all of her friends together in the shed, holding their ping-pong paddles up. Jack was pulling a funny face, and Michiko was doing bunny ears behind his head. It made Mia giggle every time she saw it. And she just knew it would still make her laugh when they opened up the time capsule ages from now.

'Mrs Bonacci?' Mia spoke up. Her voice was loud and clear. 'Can I go first?'

Mrs Bonacci looked surprised, and then she nodded.

Mia cleared her throat, and started to read. '*I don't think it matters if your friends are the same as you, or completely different, or if they're girls or boys. What matters to me is that we have fun together, we laugh together and we understand each other.*'

For a moment there was total silence. Then everyone clapped, and Michiko and Shae cheered loudly.

Wow, thought Mia happily. *That wasn't so bad!* She looked over at Jack, and he gave her the thumbs-up sign. Then he mouthed the words *Magic Mia!*

Mia grinned back. She felt great!

One by one, everyone put their tributes in the jar. Soon, there was only a handful of people left.

'It's your turn, Michiko,' said Mrs Bonacci.

Michiko held out her friendship tribute. She had decorated the edges with stars.

'My friends are like bright stars, shining in the sky,' she read. *'I am so lucky to know them! They are always there for me.'*

Then Michiko put her tribute into the jar, and everyone clapped.

'Excellent, Michiko,' smiled Mrs Bonacci. 'Now, who's left? How about you, Jack?'

Jack nodded. 'I had lots of trouble

finding a picture of all my friends together, Mrs Bonacci,' he said. 'But I finally found this one.'

Jack pulled out a picture and held it up. Everyone laughed. It was a picture of a group of monkeys, hanging from their tails. But over the monkeys' faces, Jack had stuck photos of his friends' faces instead! Oliver, Hugo and Flynn were the first three monkeys. At the end of the branch were Mia, Shae and Michiko.

Once the laughing had died down, Jack got out his tribute. He had drawn cheeky monkey faces around the writing.

'I've known some of my friends for ages,' he read. *'But some of them are pretty new. They all*

have one important thing in common, though. They are totally awesome!'

Everyone clapped loudly.

'The next time you see this you'll be about to leave primary school!' said Mrs Bonacci, as she buried the jar. 'Do you think you will have changed by then?'

Everyone was quiet for a moment. Then Jack spoke up and said exactly what Mia was thinking.

'Maybe,' he said. 'But one thing definitely won't have changed. We'll all still be friends!'

Collect them all!

go girl

Sleep-over

Boy friend?

Surf's Up

Flower Girl

Dancing Queen

Camp Chaos

Sister Spirit

Back to School

Sink or Swim

Birthday Girl

The Worst Gymnast

Music Mad

Best Christmas Ever

Class Captain

The New Girl

Karate Kicks

Secret's Out

Holiday!

Netball Dreams

The Big Split

www.gogirlhq.com

FAIRY SCHOOL Drop-out

Elly hates being a fairy – all those
itchy tutus and boring spells.
It's not nearly as fun as skateboarding.
Follow Elly the Fairy School Drop-out
on all her fabulous adventures.